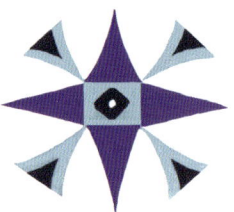

A Ring for a King

A Tale of King Solomon

Written by Martha Seif Simpson
Illustrated by D. Yael Bernhard

 Wisdom Tales

A Ring for a King: A Tale of King Solomon
Text © 2025 Martha Seif Simpson
Illustrations © 2025 D. Yael Bernhard

All rights reserved. No part of this book may be used or reproduced in any manner without written permission, except in critical articles and reviews.

Wisdom Tales is an imprint of World Wisdom, Inc.

Library of Congress Cataloging-in-Publication

Names: Simpson, Martha Seif, 1954- author. | Bernhard, Durga, illustrator.
Title: A ring for a king : a tale of King Solomon / written by Martha Seif Simpson ; illustrated by Durga Yael Bernhard.
Description: Bloomington, Indiana : Wisdom Tales, 2025. | Audience term: Children | Audience: Ages 4-8. | Audience: Grades 2-3. | Summary: Humble servant Ezra finds a ring inscribed with wise words that help King Solomon address his people.
Identifiers: LCCN 2024031204 (print) | LCCN 2024031205 (ebook) | ISBN 9781957670119 (hardback ; acid-free paper) | ISBN 9781957670126 (epub)
Subjects: CYAC: Solomon, King of Israel--Fiction. | Gifts--Fiction. | Wisdom--Fiction. | Jews--Fiction. | LCGFT: Picture books.
Classification: LCC PZ7.S6073 Ri 2025 (print) | LCC PZ7.S6073 (ebook) | DDC [E]--dc23
LC record available at https://lccn.loc.gov/2024031204
LC ebook record available at https://lccn.loc.gov/2024031205

Printed in China on acid-free paper

For information address Wisdom Tales,
P.O. Box 2682, Bloomington, Indiana 47402-2682
www.wisdomtalespress.com

For John,
with love

— MSS

For Marty
& family

— DYB

Ezra worked as a kitchen servant in the palace of King Solomon, the powerful ruler of ancient Israel.

While walking through the corridors, Ezra often overheard palace business. He listened as desperate people sought help from the wise king.

He also heard people of great wealth who boasted of their power and good fortune as they feasted.

After the crowds left, Ezra would always bring a cup of wine to the weary ruler. As the king's cup-bearer, Ezra had proven to be a trustworthy servant.

One evening, King Solomon spoke to him. "Being king isn't easy. I try to help those who are troubled. But often, I don't know what to say to ease their suffering."

"Yes, Your Majesty," said Ezra.

"And though I enjoy the lively company of noblemen, I tire of their bragging," Solomon said. "How can they not see that their success can quickly turn to failure? That good times can turn to bad?"

"But Sire, can't bad times also get better?" Ezra asked.

"Just so," said the king. "I have no trouble writing laws to govern my kingdom. Yet I struggle to find the right words to make a sad person hopeful or a proud person humble."

Ezra made a silent vow to help King Solomon.

The next day, he asked the other servants, "What would you say to make a sad person hopeful or a proud person humble?"

"We don't have time for riddles, boy," the cook said. "Take this food to the king's table."

But the heavy tray slipped from Ezra's grasp, and crashed to the kitchen floor.

"Useless boy!" the cook shouted.

"Begone!"

Ezra ran until he left the palace grounds. "My life is ruined!" he thought. Ezra slumped by the roadside, wondering how he would survive. "But perhaps, if I can find the words to help King Solomon, I may be forgiven."

Ezra asked everyone he met: "What can you say to make a sad person hopeful or a proud person humble?" Most people ignored him or shoved him aside. A few just looked puzzled. No one had an answer.

After a while, he saw a man carrying a basket of pomegranates. The man stumbled over a rock, losing his grip on the basket. Pomegranates tumbled all over the cobblestones.

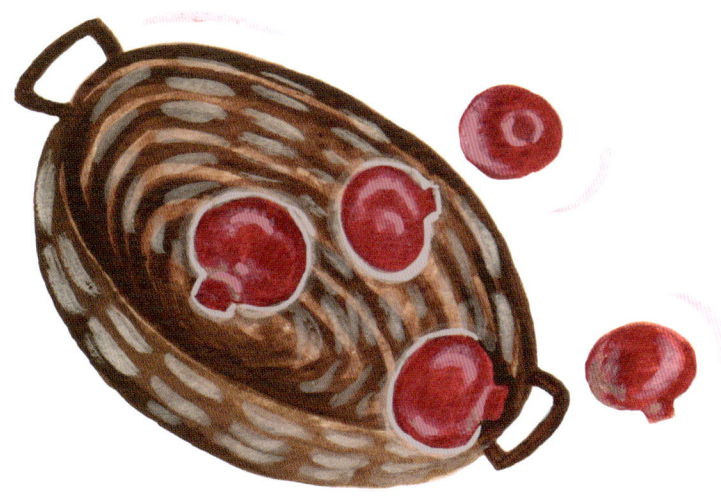

Ezra jumped up. "Here, let me help you."

"Thank you," said the man. "Is there any way I can repay your kindness?"

"I'm afraid not," Ezra said, "unless you can tell me the words that could make a sad person hopeful or a proud person humble."

The man smiled. "Perhaps I can." He took a ring from a pouch hanging on his belt. "There are letters inscribed here that have always given me comfort. Take it, and may good fortune come to you and to others who can understand its meaning."

Ezra thanked the man and ran back to the palace. He joined the line of people waiting to have an audience with King Solomon. At last, his turn came.

"Cup-bearer, what brings you here?" asked the king.

"The cook sent me away for dropping a tray," Ezra said. "But I hope to redeem myself. I have brought you a ring with a special inscription." He held it out to the surprised king, who gently took it.

King Solomon turned and turned the ring in his fingers. At first, he only saw the Hebrew letters *gimel*, *zayin*, and *yud*. Suddenly he knew what they meant and said aloud, "'*Gam Zeh Ya'avor*' — This too shall pass!"

His worried expression disappeared. "How true! Knowing that bad times are bound to end can give hope to those who suffer grief or misfortune. Yet these same words can humble the boastful by warning them that their luck could change in an instant!"

"May I be forgiven, Your Majesty, and return to the kitchen?" Ezra asked.

"Better than that," the king said. "To reward you for this great gift and your loyal service, you shall have my deepest gratitude. And a sack of gold."

So just like that, it was Ezra's life that changed for the better. Still, he vowed to remain humble, knowing that his fortunes could unexpectedly pass away.

Ezra shared his good fortune with the kind man who had given him the ring. And from then on, King Solomon always wore the ring that offered comfort and wisdom to himself and to his people.

Author's Note

The story "This Too Shall Pass," on which this book is based, has ancient origins. Some folklorists say it can be traced to 13th century Persian Sufi poet Farid ad-Din Attar of Nishapur. Others attribute it to a tale of King Solomon, who reigned in Israel from around 970 to 931 BCE. Among the many retellings is a reference from Abraham Lincoln in a campaign speech from 1859. I first heard the story as part of a rabbi's sermon.

I wrote this story in 2021, during the second year of a global pandemic. I chose to present the story from a boy's point of view to make it more accessible to a younger audience. Perhaps my version will provide some comfort and wisdom to a new generation of readers.

— Martha Seif Simpson

Artist's Note

The illustrations in this book were inspired by ancient relief sculptures, pottery, signature seals, and other artifacts in the Israel Museum, the Bible Lands Museum, and the Tower of David Museum — all in Jerusalem. Walking in the Old City on 3000-year-old cobblestones worn smooth by camels, donkeys, and sandaled feet that date back millennia, it was easy to imagine the characters in this story. Theirs was a rich and diverse society, an artist's challenge and delight to depict.

My maternal grandmother often used the expression "This too shall pass." As a child, I took it as an expression of the power of time; later I came to understand how it speaks to the unpredictable nature of life, and the importance of riding the changing tides of fate with equanimity and faith.

— D. Yael Bernhard